TUCK

by
Bob Gormley

MAPLE
PUBLISHERS

TUCKER

Author: Bob Gormley

First Published in 2022

ISBN 978-1-915492-41-8 (Paperback)

Book Cover Design, Illustrations and Layout by:
    White Magic Studios
    www.whitemagicstudios.co.uk

Published by:
    Maple Publishers
    1 Brunel Way,
    Slough,
    SL1 1FQ, UK
    www.maplepublishers.com

A CIP catalogue record for this title is available from the British Library.

INDEX

The Waterfront

On a beautiful waterfront, on a majestic river, there stands a magnificent building. It has two domed towers. On each of these towers sit the statues of two giant, strange, magical looking birds. They are unlike any other birds you will ever see.

They are the size of a dragon but don't actually look frightening.

They have huge beaks but would never peck you. Their feathers are a mixture of blue and grey and sometimes look like silver in the moonlight.

They are quite amazing and like no other birds you have ever set eyes on. The birds are called Bella and Bertie.

Bella looks out over the river to watch out for the ships and ferries.

Bertie looks out over the city; some say, to see if the pubs are open, but really, it's to watch over the people!

Some folks say that if you watch Bella and Bertie closely as the light begins to fade, you may see them move slightly or even blink.

(They say it's more like a wink than a blink!)

There are sailors who say that on dark foggy nights when their ship has difficulties entering the majestic river, from the sea, they have seen a strange giant bird swooping and soaring over their ship, helping to guide it safely into the river.

Some people say that on a clear night they have seen what appears to be strange yet magical - beautiful giant birds soaring high over the city with their feathers shimmering in the moonlight.

Some even say they have seen what looks like a young lad riding on the back of these giant birds!

On certain days, this magnificent building is invisible, some days it is not.

It's invisible to people who are in a hurry to catch the multi-coloured ferry, to get to work on time on the other side of the river and just simply rush past it. Some are simply boarding the multi-coloured ferry to enjoy a cruise on the river, to view the famous waterfront and do not have the time to look up.

But strangely enough, the very next day, the very same people may suddenly stop and look up at the beauty of the building, with the two giant birds standing proudly on their towers. Some even pause and take photographs.

On the two towers are four giant clocks which have graced the beautiful waterfront for over one hundred years. These clocks are even larger than Big Ben, the famous clock in London.

At a certain time of day, usually just as the light begins to fade, if you look carefully at the giant clockface that overlooks the river, between the numbers 5 and 6 you may see what appears to be the face of a young boy.

His name is Tucker. Tucker is watching the ships come and go and the people as they stroll along the waterfront or as they leave or board the multi-coloured ferry on the river below.

Also, as the light fades a bit more, if you look closely at the two giant birds you may notice them beginning to stir and look around.

♣ ♣ ♣

Is not Just Quite Right

As the light continues to fade, Tucker who actually lives in the clock tower, emerges through a secret door near where Bella and Bertie stand so proudly. He waves to Bella and strokes Bertie's beautiful feathers and speaks to him. Bertie ruffles his feathers and sits down. With one huge leap Tucker is on the back of the giant bird.

They sit perfectly still until all the daylight has gone, then Tucker leans forward and whispers in Bertie's ear. Bertie springs into the air and soars out towards the river, swooping over the ferry that is sailing across.

Some of the passengers just feel a breeze and some think they see a shadow of what looks like an exceptionally large bird but when they look up there is nothing to see.

Bertie soars up high and turns back towards the city, where they have fun flying between, around and over the tall buildings.

Tucker and Bertie always keep a lookout for anything or anyone that appears to be out of place. Maybe a sad, lonely looking person; a lost child. Anything that is not just quite right.

Tonight, Tucker spotted something that was not just quite right. He spoke to Bertie who nodded his head to show he had seen the same thing!

In a narrow alleyway between two tall buildings there was a large pile of old cardboard boxes. Tucker was sure he had seen something move in them.

Bertie flew lower to get a better look. He was right, the boxes moved again. Without another word Bertie dropped down, nearly throwing Tucker off his back. "Whoa, steady on, fella," he shouted, hanging on to Bertie's feathers. Tucker jumped down and told Bertie to wait there while he had a look. He made his way up the alleyway towards the pile of cardboard boxes.

When he got near, he listened and thought he could hear a sort of sobbing. As he got closer still, he could see that the sobbing was coming from an incredibly sad looking young boy.

"Hello," said Tucker. The boy, startled, sat up to see a strangely dressed young lad, not much older than himself.

♣ ♣ ♣

Trust

The boy stared at Tucker who was wearing a long heavy coat with a thick leather belt and what appeared to be riding boots. On his head, an old looking, pirate type hat. He looked like he was from another time.

"Why are you here and out so late on your own, sitting in a pile of old boxes?" asked Tucker. The boy was trying to stop sobbing, which was not easy.

He was, obviously, terribly upset over something.

"Do you want to speak to me? I will leave you alone if you want me to, I do have other things to do," said Tucker, trying to sound as if he was not really that interested why he was there.

"I am just so sad," said the boy, in between sobs.

"What's your name?" asked Tucker.

"Tom. What's yours?"

"I'm Tucker and if you want to tell me what's making you so sad, then maybe I can help you. If you want me to, that is."

"I just want to be left alone," said Tom. "That's fine, I will leave you alone but not here in this horrible alleyway," said Tucker.

Tom was staring at Tucker, who said, "Do you think you can trust me? I do not live very far from here and it's not very nice in this alleyway. We could go to where I live and I think it may take your mind off the things that are making you so sad."

Tom stared at Tucker for a while, then said, "Yes, I feel that I can trust you."

"Then let's go," said Tucker, helping Tom out of the pile of cardboard boxes.

Tucker led Tom to the end of the alleyway.

When Tom saw Bertie, who had been waiting patiently for Tucker, he froze.

"What, what is that?" he squeaked. He was not sure if he was looking at a giant beautiful bird or a friendly looking dragon. It was like something from a fairy tale.

"Let's fly," said Tucker, leaping up onto Bertie's back. "You said you trust me!"

"Yes, but I'm not getting on the back of that!"

Bertie ruffled his feathers and pulled a funny face, looking a bit offended.

"Now you've upset him. Does he look like he would hurt anyone?"

Tom looked at Bertie who sort of smiled at him in a "birdy" sort of way. Tom smiled back.

Tucker reached down, took hold of Tom's arm and pulled him up onto Bertie's back. Tom noticed that Tucker was extraordinarily strong. "Hold on tight!" shouted Tucker and with one giant leap Bertie rose into the night sky and raced out towards the river.

Tom could just not take in what was happening to him. This was just the most amazing thing you could even dream about.

Bertie swept out over the river. He could feel that Tom was sad and upset so he soared out across the river, twisting and turning, hoping the excitement of it would take Tom's mind off things for a while.

After a wild ride over the moonlit water, Bertie turned back towards the magnificent building with the two towers, on the waterfront.

Tom stopped sobbing. Even though he was so sad he knew what was happening to him was the most amazing thing that could ever happen to anyone!

♣ ♣ ♣

Tucker's Secret Room

Bertie flew twice around the high tower before landing back on his favourite spot. "Careful, climbing down," warned Tucker.

As Tom dropped to his feet, he spotted another bird, just like Bertie, sitting on the opposite tower. He was sure the bird winked at him as he followed Tucker through the secret door into the huge tower.

Tom was amazed to see that he was in a room behind one of the giant clock faces that he had seen so many times from way below.

Tom suddenly felt warm and very safe being here with Tucker. This was Tucker's room, where Tucker lived.

Tom looked around, in wonder, at some of the things in the room.

There was an incredibly old steam train, painted in beautiful, bright colours, puffing out smoke; going around the room on a track, suspended from the ceiling. It had an exceptionally large headlight, which changed colour and spread light all around this strange, yet beautiful room. As the train passed Tom, it gave a loud whistle that seemed to say, "welcome."

There were stars twinkling on the ceiling, a sun and a moon moving across the ceiling, there even appeared to be shooting stars moving in all directions.

On the walls there was a collection of old musical instruments – trumpets, fiddles, banjos, whistles and drums - all mixed up with sheets of music which looked like they had been played many times.

There were shelves full of old books. In the middle of the room stood an exceptionally large, old, wooden table which was covered with more books, paint pots, brushes, pencils and pens. In one corner was a small kitchen with a cooker that had a pot of the most wonderful smelling stew bubbling away. Tom suddenly felt very hungry. Tom looked around and realised Tucker had been watching him and smiling. "I guess you have not eaten for a while. I will get you something," said Tucker.

Tom sat at the table while Tucker fetched him a large bowl of the wonderful mouth-watering stew and a large wooden spoon to eat it with. He cut Tom the thickest slice of bread he had ever seen!

"You enjoy that and relax, then maybe we could talk but only if you want to," said Tucker. "If not, you can just finish your stew and I'll take you anywhere you want to go but not back to that horrible alleyway."

Tom finished his food in silence.

He looked at Tucker who had been watching him eat and said, "I feel I can trust you, so I'll tell you why I was in that alleyway."

Tom's Story

"I have two brothers and two sisters; my dad went away to sea months ago and we have not heard from him since. I overheard someone saying a ship had been in the middle a giant storm and may have sunk. That could be my dad's ship.

"Since then, my mum has been so sad and works awfully hard to be able to look after us. I heard her saying her prayers last night. She was crying, saying she was so scared of not being able to provide for us all.

"It was then that I thought that if I left home, it would be easier for mum with one less to feed and buy clothes for. I knew she would miss me, but I thought it would still be better for her with one less to look after.

"Maybe me leaving would help and make it that bit easier for my mum to look after my brothers and sisters."

Tucker sat looking at Tom for a while, before saying, "You know you are a daft and silly, silly boy!" Tom was surprised by what Tucker said, "What do you mean, calling me a daft, silly boy?" asked Tom.

Tucker, shaking his head, said, "Right, for a start, just look at yourself. You look well fed, clean and healthy, you are wearing good warm clothes.

"Overall, I would say your mum is doing an excellent job and managing quite well to care for her children, if you are anything to go by and yes, she will worry and pray each night that she can continue to do so.

"I would guess deep down she is very proud that she is managing at all, with your father not being there. Can you imagine how sad and scared your mum will be right now, not knowing where you are, if you are safe, thinking the worst about whether you have come to any harm or danger? Out alone in such a big city, this late and in the dark. On top of that she does not know what has happened to your father. Is he safe or in some kind of danger, would he ever come home, would she ever see him again?"

Tucker could see Tom was thinking about what he was saying.

Tom sat silently for a while then said, "I have been so silly, haven't I?"

"And daft," said Tucker, smiling.

"About your dad," asked Tucker, "how long has he been gone and where was his ship heading for?" "He has been gone for months," said Tom, "his ship was heading for America but never arrived."

Tom could see Tucker was thinking about something. "There is something I love to do at night, Tom. I go down to the docks and when a new ship arrives, Bertie and I, often, and very quietly, land on the rooftop of one of the warehouses and listen to the sailors below telling tales of their voyages and travels from all over the world. I find it fascinating to hear where they have been - the islands and different lands they have visited, storms that scared them, about seeing whales and dolphins. These old sailors have some remarkable stories to tell!

"A couple of nights ago, I was listening to sailors who had just arrived from America. They were telling a tale about passing a small island far out at sea and saying that they saw what looked like a ship, up on the beach. They said the weather was so bad and they could not see too clearly and it was too rough to stop.

"One sailor even said he thought he caught a glimpse of what could have been people on the beach near the ship but could not see clearly with the heavy rain and high waves crashing on the beach. He then said it was probably nothing, just the trees near the beach blowing in the wind."

♣ ♣ ♣

Searching

Tom could see Tucker was thinking about something. "I wonder, I just wonder," said Tucker, startling Tom by jumping to his feet, saying, "Get your coat on, Tom, we're going for a ride."

Tucker threw Tom a spare hat and scarf, "You will need these."

Before Tom knew it, Tucker was rushing him up the stairs that led to the two towers where Bertie and Bella stood.

The birds turned their huge heads to hear Tucker say, "Bella, Bertie, we have a job to do tonight. We're going out over the sea." Tucker leaped up on to Bertie's back, pulling Tom up with him and shouted to Bella, "Follow us and stay close!"

The two birds lifted off together and soared out over the river towards the open sea. They were soon in full flight, which seemed to Tom like the speed of an express train. Tom, hanging on tight to Tucker, shouted, "What are you doing, where are we going?" "Not sure yet, just hang on tight and trust me," Tucker shouted back.

They flew like the wind, on and on, further and further out over the ocean. The land behind them soon vanished into the distance.

It was a stunning starlit night with the biggest and brightest full moon you could ever see.

The stars were flashing by overhead, and the ocean racing by below them.

Tom was a little bit frightened but very, very excited too.

Tom could see Tucker and the two giant birds scanning the sea below.

After what seemed like a very long time Tucker suddenly pointed down at something.

Bella and Bertie had spotted it too. Tucker spoke to Bertie, and he dropped lower; very quickly, closely followed by Bella.

Tom could see that Tucker had spotted a small island all on its own in the middle of this huge sea.

As they dropped lower, there on the beach was what appeared to be a large ship. Tom could just make out a group of men by the ship who were all waving at them. "Down!" Tucker shouted. Bella and Bertie both glided gracefully down, landing on the beach a short distance away from the stranded ship.

The sailors quickly realised these were not planes or helicopters that had been sent to rescue them, as they first thought, but two beautiful giant birds, the likes of which they had never seen before!

Tom, at once, leapt off Bertie and started running along the beach towards the men. At exactly the same time one of the sailors ran towards Tom.

Tom's Dad swept him off his feet. They both hugged, kissed and cried in each other's arms.

Tom and his Dad Fly Home

They were left alone for a few minutes, then Tucker moved forward as the rest of the sailors did the same.

Tucker asked the sailors not to approach his birds, which were now quite busy eating the fruit from the trees along the edge of the beach.

The men asked Tucker lots of questions.

"Who are you?

How did you get here?

What are these birds?

Where have you come from?

Will you be able to save us?"

Tucker answered, "Hold on, slow down, it doesn't matter who I am or where we came from, listen to me. This is what's going to happen. I will take Tom and his father back with me now. When I get back, I will inform the Coastguard who will notify the Navy. I would guess that within a day you will all be safely rescued and heading for home. I promise you."

Tucker turned to Tom's dad and said, "You and Tom will ride back together on Bertie, I'll follow on Bella. It's a beautiful calm, moonlit night so you will be very safe, we need to be back before it gets light. You will understand why once we are back."

Tom's dad hesitated, looking at the size of Bertie. "Please just do as I ask," said Tucker. Tom added, "Come on dad, don't be afraid, you may even enjoy it."

Bertie bent lower so Tom's dad could clamber up onto his back.

Tom joined his dad and actually started instructing his dad on how to sit still and hold on tight.

Tom giving his dad instructions made Tucker smile. Tucker sprung up onto Bella and shouted to the sailors who were watching, open-mouthed, "I will send help as quickly as I can and, please, when you all get back try not to tell anyone about what you have seen tonight."

"Who would believe us anyway?!" one of the sailors shouted back.

With that the two giant birds lifted gracefully into the night sky.

They swept back along the beach, low over the sailors, who were all waving. Tom, his dad and Tucker all waved back. "I will send help, trust me," shouted Tucker.

Heading for Home

They turned and soared back the way they had come and soon vanished in the distance.

Tom's dad couldn't believe he was actually flying on such an amazing bird but was just so happy he was back with his son and heading for home!

They flew like the wind for quite a while and then suddenly Tom's dad spotted the lights of the famous waterfront and the magnificent building with its two towers. As they got closer, he noticed at once that the two giant birds were not on the towers.

He then realized that he and his son were actually riding on one of those birds.

Tucker flew alongside Tom and his dad, and shouted, "Tell Bertie where you live, he knows the city well."

As Tom's dad spoke to Bertie, they swept over the waterfront. Bertie turned and flew along the water's edge to an old part of the city.

Tucker and Bella followed closely.

Before long they dropped down and landed on the edge of a large, beautiful park, surrounded by old but very grand houses.

All three jumped to the ground together.

"That's our house," shouted Tom, excitedly pointing to a house that had a huge dog in the front bay window. The dog had seen them and barked excitedly.

The front door opened and a lady appeared, staring across at this strange sight that she couldn't quite understand.

Tom and his dad stepped out of the shadows of the trees.

They all froze for a few seconds, then Tom's Mum began to run at the same time that Tom and his dad ran to meet her.

They all fell into one another's arms and hugged for a long time.

Tom's mum asked, "But how, how can this be? I can't believe it! How is this possible?"

She then spotted Tucker, Bella and Bertie watching from under the trees. "Am I seeing things?" she asked.

"We're only here because of this young man and his amazing birds," said Tom's dad.

"Oh, thank you, thank you," exclaimed Tom's mum, flinging her arms around Tucker, giving him a huge hug. "Please come in and sit with us. I want to hear how you managed to bring the children's father home to them."

"I would love to," said Tucker, "but I must let the coastguard know right away so they can arrange for the rescue of the men still out there on the island."

Tucker called his birds out from the trees and leapt up onto Bertie. As they rose, Tucker looked down to see four children in their pyjamas and a large dog rush down the path jumping on Tom and their dad. Tucker and his birds swung back and swooped down low over the happy family. Tucker shouted, "Enjoy tonight, hope to see you all again soon."

Tom's family stood amazed by what they were seeing and waved back, shouting "Thank you, thank you."

It was by now getting brighter, so they flew as fast as possible back to the two towers on the waterfront.

The birds landed back on their towers just before it was full daylight.

♣ ♣ ♣

Sending Help

Tucker jumped down as soon as Bertie landed. He went quickly through his secret door and ran down the many flights of stairs.

He dashed over towards the river and burst into the coastguard's office.

The coastguard was a bit surprised to see this strange boy who said, "Right, no time for questions, please listen."

He reminded the coastguard about the ship, that had gone missing some months earlier, on its way to America. The coastguard said he did remember but thought that ship was lost. "Please show me your charts and I will give you the exact location of an island. There are shipwrecked sailors there who need rescuing."

The coastguard listened closely and laid out the charts and, sure enough, there was a tiny island right where Tucker was pointing.

The coastguard said he thought there was a navy ship in that area, he picked up the phone to contact them. He then turned to speak to Tucker, just to see the door closing as Tucker left.

A Job Well Done

As Tucker made his way back up to his room behind the giant clock, he knew the navy would at that moment be heading full steam for the island to save the shipwrecked sailors.

The next evening, in the dark, Bertie and Tucker sat smiling on the roof of the pier, as they watched all the rescued sailors come down the gangway to be embraced by their waiting partners and many happy children.

Lots of hugging, kissing and crying. Tucker could hear all the questions.

"How did you get rescued?"

"Who found you all?"

"This doesn't seem possible."

The answers were all the same.

"You wouldn't believe us if we told you." It made Tucker feel happy and he knew it had been a job well done, to have brought so many families safely back together.

The rest of the night passed as normal - Tucker, Bella and Bertie flying over the city. All was peaceful and quiet.

The next day was a warm sunny Saturday. Tucker looked out between numbers 5 and 6.

He saw a family below with a huge dog, all staring up at the giant clock.

He realized it was Tom with his mum, dad, brothers and sisters.

Tucker rushed down from his room behind the clock and ran outside to the family who all stood smiling with their arms outstretched.

Tucker was embraced in one big family hug mixed with tears and thanks. Even the huge dog was jumping up and licking Tucker's face.

They sat in a circle on the grass in front of the very tall building with the two birds on the towers. Tom's mum opened a huge picnic basket and they tucked into the lovely food, all asking different questions. They listened as Tucker told them how he how found Tom in the alleyway and all that followed that night.

Tom and his dad glanced up at the two giant birds that seemed to smile back at them.

Over time, Tucker would visit Tom and his family, usually after dark, so Bertie and Bella could explore the park opposite and have a nibble on the fresh grass.

Tucker grew very close to the family and spent many happy times with them.

For some time afterwards, on and around the waterfront and the docks, some of the sailors who had been rescued, could be heard telling tales about a young boy and two giant birds that helped to save them.

"You sailors do tell some strange stories," was the usual reply amid the laughter.

But the rescued sailors knew the truth. They never again passed the magnificent, tall building with the two very unusual birds sitting on their towers without stopping to salute those birds, who appeared to smile back and wink in a "birdy" sort of way.

Now and again, they would wave up to a young boy whose face they could see between the numbers 5 and 6 on the giant clock face.

Tom never ran away from home again.

Lightning Source UK Ltd.
Milton Keynes UK
UKHW020853161122
412247UK00011B/245

9 781915 492418